The Sandwich

by

Ian Wallace and Angela Wood

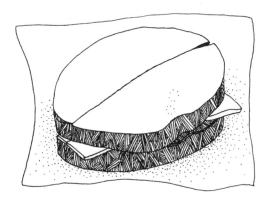

Canadian Cataloguing in Publication Data

Wallace, Ian, 1950-
    The sandwich

ISBN 0-919964-02-8 pa.

I. Wood, Angela, 1951-   II. Title.

PS8595.A44S26   jC813'.54   C75-10788-X
PZ7.W34Sa

Printed and Bound in Canada

Kids Can Press
585 1/2 Bloor Street West
Toronto, Ontario M6G 1K5

75 0

Milgrom's Variety
SCHOOL SUPPLIES

PATENT MEDICINES BABY NEEDS

COSMETICS PERFUMES FILMS

for our parents
Kathleen
and Robert
Elvira and Bill

thanks to
Rosanna,
Ron and
Adrian.

'My name is Vincenzo Ferrante and I am in Grade 2 at Clinton Street Public School. I live at 538 Manning Avenue in a flat over Milgrom's Variety with my father, my sister Lisa, my Nonna, Zio Salvatore, and my two rabbits, Tucci and Zeppo. They live in a wire and wood cage that Papa and I made for them.

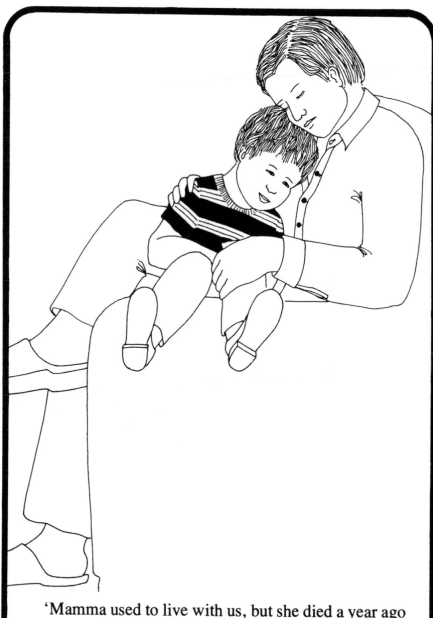

'Mamma used to live with us, but she died a year ago which makes me sad sometimes. When I'm unhappy I climb into my father's lap and feel much better.

'After Mamma's death, Nonna came over from Italy and has been helping Papa to care for Lisa and me. Every Sunday she takes us to see him at work, driving his streetcar up and down St. Clair Avenue. She helps me make my bed, cooks our favorite things to eat, and tells us bedtime stories in Italian because Nonna can't speak English.

'Until today I have always eaten lunch at home. Tomorrow for the first time I am going to eat at school. Mamma and Nonna would say, ''Vincenzo, you can get a better lunch at home than out of a bag. So, you'll eat at home.''

'Nonna is sick and was taken to the Toronto General Hospital so she can get better. Mrs. Leone next door is going to take care of Lisa until Papa gets home from work. Zio Salvatore will take care of himself. He sleeps all day and works all night at the ice cream factory.'

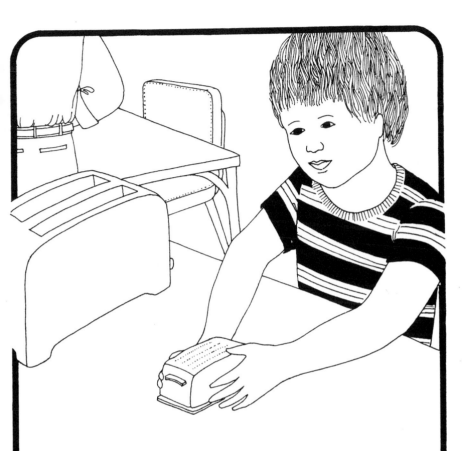

'Papa, can I butter the bread?' asked Vincenzo, climbing into his chair at the kitchen table.

'If you want, Vincenzo. That would be a big help. Here's a knife and the butter is on the counter beside the toaster.'

Returning to the table he watched intently as his
father held the bread with one hand and cut thick
slices with skill and ease.

'This is very good bread, Vincenzo, fresh out of Fiore's oven. It's the best bread in Toronto!'

'You always say that Fiore's is the best bread in Toronto, Papa.'

'Well, it is good. Isn't it?'

'Yeah, but I haven't tasted any other!' said Vincenzo, spreading the knife across a slice of bread. 'How's this?'

'Good. Very good. Now, what kind of sandwich do you want, provolone cheese, mortadella, meatballs or salami?'

'What are you going to have for your lunch, Papa?'

'Hmmmm. Let's see. Meatballs are good, but the bread becomes soggy if it turns hot outside. Salami?...Uhn...Not tomorrow. Mortadella and provolone. Such an aroma! Here, Vincenzo, taste this. Good, eh?...Now, that's what I'll have.'

'Me too, Papa. That's what I want. Mortadella and provolone, just like you!' Vincenzo placed the thin slices of mortadella carefully on the bread as his father cut the provolone.

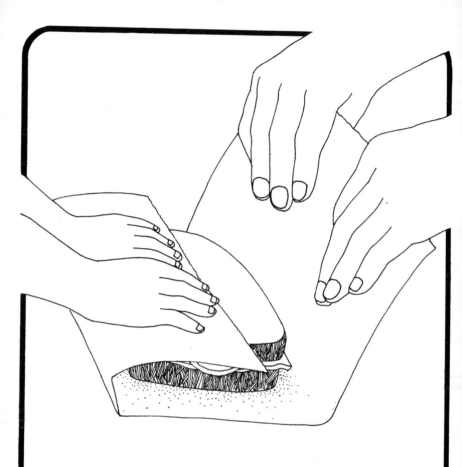

'There we are, Vincenzo. This slice goes on top and we are done. Will you hand me the wax paper? Now, if you hold this end down I'll fold the other ends over.'

'Can we have some anisette cookies and a can of orange juice with our lunch, Papa?'

'If that's what you want, then that's what we'll have.'

Together they filled their brown lunch bags; first the mortadella and provolone sandwich and then the anisette cookies, also wrapped in wax paper. The can of orange juice was placed on its side and the top of the bag folded down.

'It's getting late, Vincenzo, so off to bed you go. Wash your face and hands and remember both sides. Brush your teeth, go to the bathroom and I will be in to say goodnight.'

'Okay, Papa. But will you tell me a story about when you were a little boy?'

'If you promise to go right to sleep. And remember, just one.'

His lunch bag in one hand and school books in the other, Vincenzo raced down the two flights of stairs to the street below. The sun was shining on his face and he felt good inside.

'Today,' he said to a passing squirrel, 'I am going to eat in the cafeteria and are we going to have fun!'

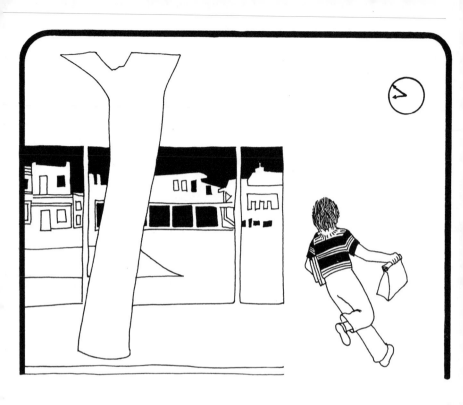

The clock ticked and ticked and ticked, but the morning seemed like it would never end. Watching its measured movements made Vincenzo's eyes blurr. His stomach began to groan and toss, signalling eleven-thirty.

riiiiinnnnggg
twelve o'clock

jump

scramble

"WALK don't _run!_"

giggle

snort

and

roar

desk..row...teacher...door...

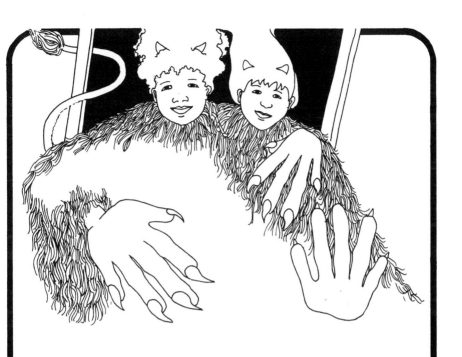

'Vincenzo!' shouted Matt. 'Come'n eat with us!'
'Okay,' he replied, running towards his friend.
Matt threw an arm around Vincenzo's shoulder
and like a two-headed monster they strutted down the
hall. Hans, Cindy, Rita, and Paul were waiting at the
table by the window. Vincenzo dropped his lunch on
the table and sat on the end of the bench beside Rita.

'Vincenzo,' she asked, 'how's your Nonna today?'

'She's still sick. Papa took her to the hospital yesterday. That's why I am eating here instead of at home.'

'She'll get better,' assured Rita. 'Don't worry. At least you get to eat lunch with us!'

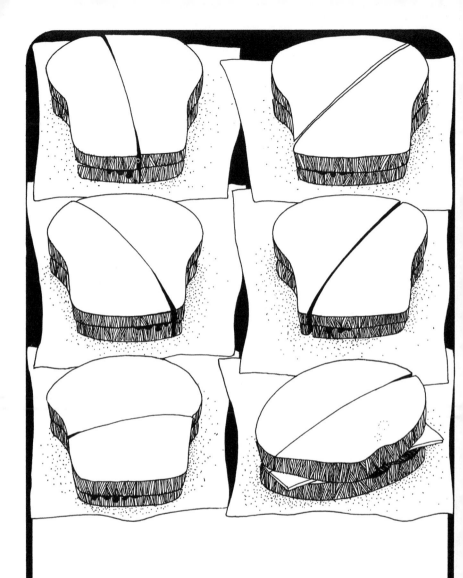

Vincenzo turned and glanced around the table at the lunches which were now coming out of their bags.

'They're all the same except mine,' he whispered to himself.

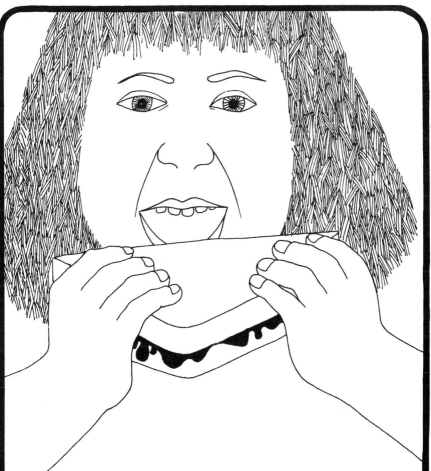

'Peanut butter and jam is my favourite sandwich,'
stated Paul.

'Mine too,' said Rita, holding hers in front of her
face. 'I won't eat any other sandwich and that makes
my mother so mad. She says that someday I am going
to turn into a peanut! That would be neat, eh?'

'Yeah. Rita the Peanut,' giggled Cindy.

Everyone nodded, laughing.

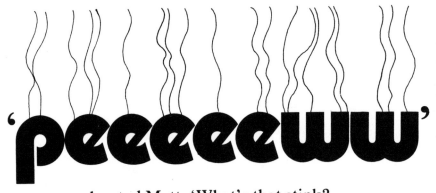

'**peeeeeww**'

shouted Matt, 'What's that stink?
I've never smelled anything like it at
our table before.'

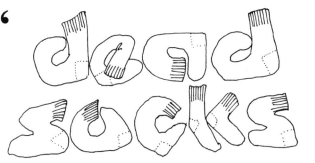

' **dead socks** '

screeched Rita, grabbing her nose.
Heads turned, sniffing back and
forth, up and down.

'Vincenzo.' sniffed Matt. 'It's Vincenzo's sandwich!'

His friends covered their noses and began to laugh.

'Vincenzo eats stinky meat!' laughed Matt.

'Vincenzo eats stinky meat!' sang Rita, Hans,
Paul, and Cindy.

'Vincenzo eats stinky meat!' rang throughout the
cafeteria.

Vincenzo didn't sing or laugh. He dropped his head onto his chest and wiped away the stinging in his eyes. The sandwich was staring him in the face. With one quick movement, he grabbed it and shoved it into the bag.

'The garbage,' he thought, 'that's where it belongs and then I can run out of the cafeteria!'

But he didn't run outside. His friends, finishing their lunch, went into the schoolyard to play tag. They'd asked him to come along, but he didn't want to go. Instead, he sat alone for the remainder of the lunch hour. He returned to the classroom and quickly shoved the lunch into his desk.

'No one will see or smell it there,' he thought.

The afternoon passed even more slowly than the morning.

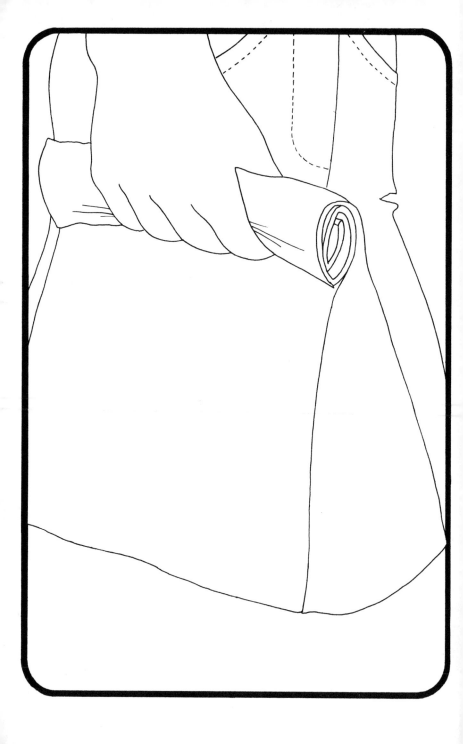

When Vincenzo returned home that day his father noticed that he was still carrying his lunch.

'Vincenzo,' asked his father, 'what did you eat for lunch?'

'Nothing.'

'Nothing! You took a good lunch to school and ate nothing? What's the matter, are you sick?'

'No, Papa, I'm not sick. I didn't feel like eating, that's all.'

'The day that you don't eat your lunch, Vincenzo, there *is* something wrong. Please, tell me what it is!'

Vincenzo shifted his weight from one foot to the other and back again. His left hand moved across his face and stopped behind his ear where it began to scratch.

'My friends ... Umm .. they .. uh .. laughed at my sandwich and shouted, "Vincenzo eats stinky meat!"

'Ohhh,' sighed his father. 'So that's it. Come here.'

Vincenzo climbed into his father's lap as he had done many times before and waited for him to speak.

'Why do you think they laughed at you?'

'Because my sandwich stinks, that's why! But it is a good sandwich, isn't it?'

'Do you like mortadella and provolone, Vincenzo?'

'Yes, Papa, I do.'

'Then it is a good sandwich. Your friends laughed because it was different. It smelled strange, looked different, and it was new to them.'

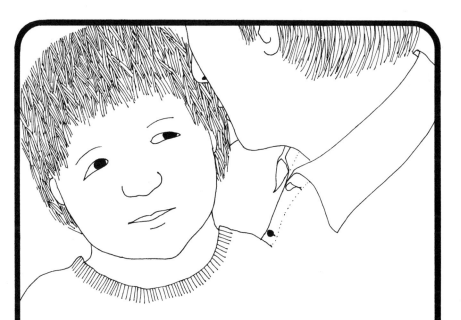

'Are you sure?' asked Vincenzo, doubtfully.

'Yes, son, I'm sure. Tomorrow when you go to school and your friends laugh at your sandwich, you laugh with them. Then they won't laugh any more.' He paused, 'That is, if you want to take another mortadella and provolone sandwich to school. Or would you like me to buy you some peanut butter and jam?'

Vincenzo sat still and thoughtful in his father's arms and then answered, 'No Papa, you don't have to buy me peanut butter and jam. I'll take my own sandwich.'

'Good, Vincenzo. Always remember, you are who you are and you have nothing to be ashamed of. Now, will you help me get supper ready?'

'Sure!'

Late that night, he dreamed. He was seated at a table twelve feet high in the middle of a large room while bears danced around the walls. There, set in front of him, was the biggest and most beautiful jar of peanut butter and jam that he had ever seen. With a large gold knife, he dug into the glass jar and spread a huge brown and red glob across a slice of bread. He smiled down with delight at his family who looked very sad and kept eating and eating and eating.

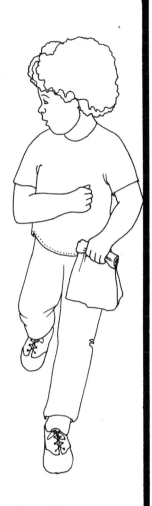

'Vincenzo, why are you taking so long?'

'I'll be there in a minute, Matt. You go ahead.'

'Hurry up, then. We have to eat fast so we can play outside longer,' shouted Matt, racing off down the hall.

When Vincenzo reached the cafeteria table, his friends were seated as they had been the day before.

'Vincenzo,' asked Matt, 'what did you bring for lunch today? Something stinkless I hope.'

Everyone laughed, except Vincenzo.

'No,' he replied firmly, 'I have stinky meat and cheese.'

'Oh no. Vincenzo eats stinky meat again,' groaned Rita, grabbing her nose, 'and I have to sit beside him!'

Matt laughed, and Rita laughed, as did Hans, Cindy, and Paul. But louder than them all laughed Vincenzo.

'I eat stinky meat!' he shouted at the top of his lungs.

Startled, his friends looked towards him.

'I dare you to eat some peanut butter and jam!'
blurted Cindy.

'I don't want your peanut butter and jam. I have my
own sandwich that my Papa and I made.'

'I dare you!' threatened Matt. 'I dare you!'

Vincenzo glanced around the table and met five pairs of eyes staring into his. He felt sweaty all over and wondered if it showed on his face.

'No,' he thought, 'I won't take a dare,' and took a big bite into his sandwich and another bite and another.

His friends sat and watched in amazement. Vincenzo was eating a stinky meat sandwich and seemed to like it!

Everyone began to eat except Matt who stared intently at the other half of Vincenzo's sandwich. Slowly, his arm crept across the table and, picking the sandwich up with one hand, lifted it to his mouth. There it sat for a few moments. He closed his eyes tightly and took a bite.

Vincenzo, seeing what had happened, smiled to himself.

'Papa was right,' he thought.

Arm over arm and hand over hand the stinky meat sandwich moved around the table. It reached its way to Rita who took a bite, chewed, and stopped.

'It's not bad. It's not bad!' she whispered to Paul and handed the one small bite left to Vincenzo. He popped it into his mouth and reached into his lunch bag for the anisette cookies and orange juice.